The Rhymachine of Rufus McLean

Written by Quentin Flynn
Illustrated by Ian Forss

Contents

Meet the Characters

Rufus McLean

An inventor.

Fingus the Wee

A sheep-stealer.

Bogie Duntroon

A haggis-smuggler.

Lochless McDilly

A would-be restaurant owner.

Macrascal, McSlimy, MacSnortle, McCrackle and Campbell

The other Highland lairds.

Dear Reader

On a dark Scottish night, the dastardly Highland lairds have their usual agenda of haggis-rustling, pick-sporraning and oatcake-smuggling ruined by some unwelcome news. They are required to do something they never expected – and they will need some serious help to accomplish their awful task!

Quentin Flynn
Author

The Scottish Highlands

1. Castle Campbell
2. Castle McCrackle
3. Castle MacSnortle
4. Castle McSlimy
5. Castle McLean
6. Castle Wee
7. Castle McDilly
8. Castle Duntroon
9. Castle Macrascal

1 A Highland Gathering

Wee: SMALL *or* little

Wallydraigle: A FEEBLE, *weak* PERSON

Fingus the Wee raised one quivering eyebrow impossibly high, fixing the target of his taunt with an eye so bloodshot it matched the red of his clan tartan.

"OCH, BOGIE, YOU'RE A WALLYDRAIGLE!"
he roared, with a drizzle of spit and splutter that rained over the rough wooden table.

Fingus the Wee, the shortest and fiercest sheep-stealer north of the River Spey in Scotland, stood one-and-a-half magnificent metres tall, and sported a mane of black hair like the scorched head of a woolly mammoth.

It was 1746 and Fingus the Wee was engaging in his favourite Highland sport – trading insults across the table with his red-bearded, six-foot-tall, haggis-smuggling cousin, Bogie Duntroon.

Bogie's retort echoed around the soot-stained walls of the banquet chamber in which he, Fingus the Wee, and seven other fearsomely frowning Scotsmen were feasting on deliciously stinky smoked herrings and lumpy, warm porridge.

"A wallydraigle? Weak, am I? Ye ... ye ... bletherskate!"

Bogie snorted so furiously that green slime sprayed all over Fingus's hair. His fishy breath threatened to blow out the thick, spluttering candle casting shadows across the other diners devouring their dinner.

Bogie turned to a ferocious black-haired man on his left, Rufus McLean, who was hungrily elbowing his way towards the porridge bowl. "Rufus!" he said, poking his neighbour.

Only a brave man would do that to Rufus McLean, especially when he was armed with a particularly squiffy herring.

"I've heard our enemies, the cowardly English soldiers, have been comin' to me wee cousin Fingus on their hands an' knees!" said Bogie, stroking his red beard thoughtfully.

"Oh, aye?" burped Rufus.

His heavy, black eyebrows furrowed in concentration. "Hands and knees?"

Rufus McLean was the cleverest of the chieftains when it came to inventing machines to cut gold coins in half to double his money, or to fill rolls of roast beef with stones so they could charge the English more for them, but he was a little slow to get jokes. He was the one who always needed them explained.

Fingus the Wee broke in, glaring at Bogie. "Aye?" he blustered, suddenly suspicious of his cousin's incessant teasing. "What's wrong with that?" If there was anything guaranteed to ignite the Wee's fiery temper, it was a joke about his height. He shoved his wooden bowl of porridge to one side, ready to lunge at Bogie. Bogie didn't blink.

"They've been on their hands an' knees, peerin' under his bed, asking him to come out an' fight like a man!" hooted Bogie.

The table erupted in laughter. Fingus's face relaxed and he grinned into his bowl of smoked fish and porridge.

"Right unfriendly, them English," growled Rufus, spitting out a herring bone.

"Oh, aye?" chomped Fingus across the table, crunching his way through a fish tail.

"Aye," nodded Rufus. "I went doon to London one night."

"And?" queried Bogie.

"They spent the whole night bangin' on the doors an' the walls an' the ceilin' o' me room," Rufus continued, through a mouthful of mangled fish guts.

"Really?" whistled Fingus.

He eagerly shovelled another spoonful of porridge into his mouth.

"Aye," replied Rufus, with a rare twinkle in his eye. "At three in the mornin', they were bangin' so hard, I could hardly hear meself practisin' me bagpipes!"

Fingus the Wee guffawed so hard that the porridge and fish almost came out of his nose.

A chair scraped backwards across the stony floor and the men swivelled their shaggy eyebrows towards the head of the table. A stern-looking, white-haired man rose from his seat and, after a satisfied chorus of muffled, last-minute burps, the Highlanders fell silent. The chieftain of the Campbell clan formally called the weekly meeting of the lairds to order.

"Duntroon, Macrascal, McSlimy, McDilly, McLean, MacSnortle, McCrackle and Wee! In addition to our porridge and our herrings, the Campbells offer you our greetings!

"This evening, we have our usual dastardly agenda of haggis-rustling, pick-sporraning, and oatcake-smuggling to discuss." There was a murmur of approval from the men.

"But, my ferociously feckless lairds, there is another matter which we must discuss – one of vital importance, and one that we ignore at our peril," continued Campbell.

In unison, Duntroon, Macrascal, McSlimy, McDilly, McLean, MacSnortle, McCrackle and Wee raised quivering right eyebrows like a sea of furry caterpillars attempting synchronised swimming.

"The fearsomely fickle Mrs Campbell," continued the chieftain, "has reminded me that it is Valentine's Day in only three weeks and that she expects us all to do something romantic for our dearly beloved wives!"

At the mention of their dearly beloved wives, the faces gathered around the table looked startled, and eight eyebrows continued to quiver in alarm.

"Impossible," blurted Fingus the Wee in horror. "I canna be romantic to me dearly beloved wife! Why, that's askin' for trouble, like ticklin' the Loch Ness monster!"

"Romantic?" growled Bogie Duntroon suspiciously. "This Valentine laddie is no' a

Scotsman, is he? I say we skewer him with a sharp caber and toss the pair o' useless sticks in the loch!"

Campbell raised his hands. "There's no need for panic," he reassured the nervous chieftains. "Apparently, we only have to be romantic for a day. And we have three weeks to think of something romantic to do. It shouldn't be *that* impossible."

Around the wooden table, there were grimaces, wrinkled noses and furrowed foreheads. Each of the men was thinking exactly the same thing: "It shouldn't be impossible ... but there's a whisperin' in me head tellin' me it will be!"

Caber: a long *heavy* wooden **pole**

Loch: lake

2 A Worrying Problem

Skirlie: oats AND *onions* FRIED in butter

Later that week, Rufus McLean was hungrily tucking into a bowl of breakfast skirlie when he heard an insistent knocking on his castle door.

After plucking a particularly stringy piece of onion from his beard, he peered out of the window. Through swirling flurries of February snow, he recognised Fingus the Wee, looking agitated and hopping from foot to foot.

Fingus waved impatiently. "Rufus, yer bottom's hangin' out the window. Ooh, no, sorry,

it's yer face," he giggled. "Anyway, let me in because I canna reach the door handle!"

"Yer a numpty," replied Rufus with a grin. "And a full-sized one at that!" He pulled a rope hanging from the ceiling, and the machine he'd cleverly invented to open the door when he needed to urgently whisk stolen haggis, kidnapped English princesses or second-hand herrings into his castle whirred into action.

Fingus's footsteps clumped up the staircase. "Aye, some men call ye clever, Rufus McLean," he puffed when he finally reached the top of the stairs. "But others are happier tellin' the truth."

"It's grand to see you too, Fingus the Wee," snorted Rufus, ignoring his insult. "Well, at least the bottom half of ye. Where did ye leave the rest?"

Instead of retorting, Fingus swept a handful of herring bones off a stool next to Rufus McLean's breakfast table and climbed atop it.

"I'm worried about this Valentine's Day silliness," Fingus declared, scratching his purple nose nervously. "It's been keepin' me awake worse than a gutful of week-ol' oysters."

"Mrs McLean is gettin' bold an' all," sighed Rufus. "She's been scrawlin' bright red circles round me Book o' Days all week, and wanderin' round with a look

like a herring that's been eatin' mustard."

"Och, ye do have a romantic turn o' phrase," said Fingus wistfully. "Can ye no' invent a romantical machine?" he asked. "We've seen ye build all sorts o' leery fidgets an' widgets for diddlin' the English out o' their money, but this Valentine's calamity is turnin' into a matter o' life or death!"

Both men thought glumly for a minute. "I could try buildin' a wart-scratcher for the lovely ladies," suggested Rufus. "Or a wee toenail box to keep their clippin's in, instead o' scatterin' 'em through the bedsheets."

Fingus the Wee stroked his eyebrows, deep in thought. "That's maybe no' the impression to give, Rufus," he decided eventually. "I've been readin' the *Encyclopaedia Scottica* those castle-to-castle salespeople sold me last year, an' apparently ladies prefer things like flowers an' stuff."

"Flowers?" blurted Rufus in surprise. "Why would they want flowers when there's perfectly good porridge and skirlie on the table?"

"Apparently they're nae for eatin', Rufus. They just put 'em in a jar an' watch 'em."

Fingus and Rufus looked at each other, shrugging their shoulders in disbelief.

"And poems," said Fingus after a minute's contemplation. "Rhymin' bits o' sentences where ye canna be bothered finishin' yer writin' with proper full stops."

"Oh, I know about them," nodded Rufus, inadvertently dipping his beard into the remains of his breakfast. He cleared his throat:

"Black puddin' for breakfast,
with haggis an' egg,
an' a dollop of porridge beneath.
There's nary a bone,
or a seed to be found,
so what's that stuck in me teeth?"

Fingus grinned, and Rufus continued his poetic recital:

"With breath like a walrus,
an' gurglin' guts,
upon my breakfast, I munch.
And if I feel queasy,
an' bring 'er all up,
I'll 'ave it again for lunch."

Rolling with laughter, Fingus toppled off his stool and hit the floor with a thump. Undeterred, Rufus McLean was suddenly struck by a thought. "When's our next meetin' with Duntroon, Macrascal, McSlimy, McDilly, MacSnortle, McCrackle and Campbell?" he asked.

Yersel':
yourself

Fingus the Wee picked himself up and counted off his fingers. "That'll be Friday," he replied.

"Well, there's no' a moment to waste!" declared Rufus. "Let yersel' out, Fingus, this clever inventor has some clever inventin' to do."

3 A Dastardly Invention

Bogie Duntroon groaned and held the sides of his enormous belly.

"Lochless, ye gangrel, I hope ye'll be feedin' us tonight. Me tummy's as empty as the space 'tween an Englishman's ears!"

It was Lochless McDilly's turn to host the weekly meeting of the lairds, and all except Rufus McLean were seated around his table.

McDilly grinned at Bogie Duntroon. "Hungry, are ye?" he winked. "I'm experimentin' with fast fryin' up some long slivers o' tattie."

Gangrel: a DOWN *and out* **layabout**

Tattie: *potato*

Across the table, Bogie smacked his lips. "Fried tatties, eh? Here, Lochless, ye could call 'em 'Scotch fries'," he suggested helpfully.

"I'm considerin' puttin' a slice o' haggis 'tween two bread buns, too," said McDilly, winking. "I'm going to call it a 'Big McDilly'. I reckon if I start up a chain o' fast fryin' restaurants sellin' Big McDillys 'n' fries, I'll make meself a fortune!"

"It'll ne'er work, Lochless," declared Bogie, shaking his head. "Why would anyone pay perfectly good money for a feed when they can just boil up a pot o' porridge?"

There was a sudden crash, as the door to the banquet room swung open. Rufus McLean struggled in, carrying an enormous contraption swathed in a moth-eaten tartan kilt.

He dropped it breathlessly in the middle of the table, and the plates and knives on either side bounced and crashed like a dozen shimmering tambourines.

"I call it a 'pee-cee'," he declared to the dumbstruck gathering. "That's short for 'Poem Constructor'."

The collective right eyebrows of the other eight men started dancing wildly above their wide eyeballs.

"Ye said ye wanted something to keep the ladies happy while they're thinking o' this dastardly Valentine laddie. Well, cast yer peepers o'er this!"

With a dramatic flourish, Rufus McLean swept off the tartan kilt, revealing the curious contraption and flinging a cloud of dust and flakes from old moth wings throughout the room.

In the middle of the table sat a weird-looking collection of levers, buttons and slots encased in slabs of wood that were held together by alarmingly rusty kilt pins. A tatty box of rough wooden squares sat on the top of the machine.

Fingus the Wee peered nervously over the top of the table, his eyes swivelling left, then right, as if he was waiting for something to happen. "I'm no' feeling any more romantic yet," he whispered to Bogie Duntroon. "What's supposed to 'appen?"

Rufus McLean fixed Fingus with a piercing eye. "It's nae turned on, ye wallydraigle! So don't entertain ideas of kissin' us all with yer scratchy whiskers just yet."

He plonked himself on a stool and explained how his romantical invention worked: "Ye scribble romantic words on these wooden blocks, then ye pop 'em in the slots. When ye press this 'n' this 'n' this, me pee-cee starts jigglin' 'em all around inside with some other words I prepared earlier. Did ye wanna give 'er a go?"

"As long as Fingus promises not to surprise me with a slobberin' kiss when yer pee-cee's done," said Bogie Duntroon nervously.

Fingus poked out his tongue, and Rufus tossed each man a blank wooden square. "Write down the most romantic thing ye can think o', and when yer done, put yer square in the slots," he said.

The men looked bewildered, and stared at their blank squares with puzzled expressions fixed across their grubby, whiskery faces.

"If ye canna think o' something romantic, write down something that ye think will make the ladies smile."

That wasn't any easier for the Highlanders huddling around the table but, with eyes squinting, tongues hanging out, and Fingus the Wee dribbling into his beard, they set to work thinking hard.

Finally, Bogie Duntroon let out a puff of breath and scribbled some words on his square. Then, Fingus's eyes lit up and he, too, scribbled something

on his square. With agonising concentration, Macrascal, McSlimy, McDilly, McLean, MacSnortle, McCrackle and Campbell all managed to scrawl something on their squares.

The men looked relieved when their ordeal was over. "I've still no desire to be kissin' any o' ye!" complained Fingus. "Are ye sure this contraption is workin', Rufus?"

"It makes poems, not potions, ye wee rat's raisin," snorted McLean. He leant over the pee-cee, pushed some buttons, and turned a handle on the side. Inside the wooden box, the men could hear something tumbling about, and their eyes widened and eyebrows lifted in a mixture of fear and anticipation.

Finally, Rufus Mclean finished cranking the handle of the pee-cee and gave the entire machine a hearty thump. The machine let out a sound like a handful of oyster shells being dropped into a porridge bowl, and Rufus beamed. "Are ye ready?" he asked.

The men weren't completely sure what they were ready for, but they nodded anyway.

From the bottom of the pee-cee, Rufus carefully slid out a tray, upon which the small wooden squares the men had written on were interspaced with other small squares, each displaying a word.

"It looks like ye've cooked us a tray o' shortbread biscuits," marvelled Lochless McDilly. "I could use one o' them contraptions in me restaurants!"

"Yer a numpty," scowled Rufus. "Look a' the squares, ye bampots. They're writin' out a wee poem!"

Slowly, as they gazed at the tray of squares, the men realised that the words were indeed arranged into lines. Their mouths worked in unison as they silently read out the words. Then, as each man finished reading, he slumped back in his chair, looking at Rufus McLean in amazement. "That's incredible," said Bogie Duntroon. "Let me read it again." This time he read each line out loud:

"Ye smell like a kipper, yer hair is like string,
yer face looks like porridge with lumps.
Ye sound like a crow that's swallowed a stone,
yer ankles are thick like tree stumps.
Like a bumblin' bee, yer hard to ignore,
when ye give me a sting in me tummy.
Ye burp like a sailor an' snore like a boar,
ye kinda remind me o' Mummy."

Fingus the Wee could no longer contain himself. "That's the most beautiful thing I e'er heard," he blubbered, using a grubby sleeve to smear a tear from his eye.

"Which one o' ye wrote 'sting in me tummy'?" asked Rufus, trying to suppress a sniffle.

"Ye said to write something that gives the wife a smile, an' a bee buzzin' down me shirt ne'er fails with Mrs Campbell," said Campbell in a quivering voice.

The men looked at each other proudly. With the help of the rhyming machine of Rufus McLean, they'd written a romantic poem. With a scraping of chair legs, they all stood up and gave each other huge hugs. "Now it's workin'!" said Fingus the Wee, as he planted a huge, sloppy kiss on Bogie Duntroon's cheek.

4 Pee-Cee Poetry

As Valentine's Day approached, each man worked feverishly with Rufus McLean and his pee-cee to write poems for their own wives.

Like the fine piece of machinery that it was, the pee-cee worked tirelessly to construct poems that made the Highlanders feel all warm and gooey inside.

"Aye, she'll love it," declared Lochless McDilly, as he read over the final draft of the romantic poem the machine had written for his wife. Rufus McLean nodded, picked up the pee-cee's tray and read out McDilly's poem:

"Ye gobble me tatties, me haggis an' buns,
ye remind me o' pigs eatin' swill.
Ye've swelled like a bread roll,
that's baked in me oven,
and still ye have space left to fill.

Ye swallow yer pickle and slurp on yer drink,
ye burp like a bonny Scotch toad.
An' if ye can't walk far,
to cook up yer dinner,
another McDilly's is o'er the road."

"It's perfect," declared Rufus. "Now I've got to ride o'er to Fingus the Wee's castle to do one for him." He gathered up the pee-cee and thumped his way towards the door, leaving a delighted Lochless McDilly behind.

Fingus the Wee had a lump in his throat.

"Yer eyes are like turnips, yer earwax is brown,
yer teeth, they are five shades of green.
Yer moustache, it waves, like weeds in a puddle,
it's the best on a lady I've seen.

An' aye, when ye cackle, the birds all take flight
and the fat on yer arms starts a-jigglin'.
When the ground starts to shake,
like a Highland earthquake,
I know that it's just ye a-gigglin'."

"That'll be grand for me dearly beloved wifey," proclaimed Fingus, trying to swallow his emotion. "I reckon everyone's going to want one of those pee-cees one day," he said. "They'll save an awful lot o' bother."

Bogie Duntroon was next on Rufus McLean's list of romantic Highland chieftains to visit. "I've made a list of all the romantic things I've thought of that I want to put in me poem," Bogie said, after Rufus had set the pee-cee on the table with a resounding crash.

Rufus looked over the list, which was splattered with droplets of crusty, dried skirlie, and nodded approvingly. He scribbled the words onto the wooden tablets and dropped them into the slots. The handle cranked and the tablets tumbled around.

"Let me see!" said Bogie when Rufus pulled the tray of poetry out from under the pee-cee.

"Like a splutterin' bagpipe in need of a squeeze,
'neath me armpit, ye fit nice and snug.
Yer lumpy, yer dumpy,
yer've no' got much mould,
like the last sack o' spuds that I dug.
With a temper like thunder, ye boom and ye flash,
yer me rain, me drizzle, me snow.
Like a dinghy that's moored to a ruddy great post,
you're there, where'er I go.

Dirk:
a CEREMONIAL *Scottish* dagger

"Now don' be tellin' everyone I'm a romantic at heart, Rufus McLean," said Bogie, who was feeling a little embarrassed by the magnificent emotions that his poem had stirred in his heart. "Or I'll be usin' me dirk to plunder yer guts."

"I'll nae breath a word," Rufus reassured him. "The fact that yer as soft as a steamed puddin' is a secret that's safe with me."

Rufus McLean visited all of the chieftains in turn, and each day his rhyming machine cranked out enough poems to melt the heart of even the iciest chieftain's wife.

Safe in the knowledge that each and every chieftain had a romantic poem guaranteed to make this Valentine's Day one they'd never forget, Rufus rode his horse homewards along the snowy banks of a steely grey loch. "There'll be such warm hearts all through the land that I expect there'll be spring bulbs poppin' up here tomorrow," he chuckled to his horse.

5 Declarations of Love

Throughout the Highland valleys and glens, the castles of the clans Duntroon, Macrascal, McSlimy, McDilly, McLean, MacSnortle, McCrackle, Campbell and Wee awoke slowly to a morning filled with sleety snow and howling winds.

A week ago, each of the lairds had been filled with dread at the thought of having to do something, anything, romantic for Valentine's Day. Now that the day had finally arrived, they could hardly wait to leap out of bed.

One by one, in nine castles up and down the Highlands, the chieftains picked their noses, scrubbed their warts, rubbed the biggest lumps of muck from between their toes and admired themselves in the mirror.

Then, they pulled on their boots, hitched up their kilts and excitedly clattered their way downstairs to their sculleries, where Mrs Wee, Mrs Duntroon, Mrs Macrascal, Mrs McSlimy, Mrs McDilly, Mrs McLean, Mrs MacSnortle, Mrs McCrackle and Lady Campbell had been working since the sun came up.

"Top o' the morn to ye," boomed Bogie Duntroon to Mrs Duntroon, who whirled around in alarm. It wasn't yet half-past eleven. What on earth was her husband doing out of bed so early? And why was his eyebrow twitching so nervously?

It was a scene that was repeated up and down the Highlands. Unfortunately, after each of the McRomeos had read out their magnificently poetic declarations of love, another scene was repeated up and down the Highlands. It was, the men decided later, not quite the scene that they had expected.

"Ye gobble me tatties, me haggis an' buns,
ye remind me o' pigs eatin' swill.
Ye've swelled like a bread roll,
that's baked in me oven,
and still ye have space left to fill.

Ye swallow yer pickle and slurp on yer drink,
ye burp like a bonny Scotch toad.
An' if ye can't walk far,
to cook up yer dinner,
another McDilly's is o'er the road."

"Yer eyes are like turnips, yer earwax is brown,
yer teeth, they are five shades of green.
Yer moustache, it waves, like weeds in a puddle,
it's the best on a lady I've seen.

An' aye, when ye cackle, the birds all take flight,
and the fat on yer arms starts a-jigglin'.
When the ground starts to shake,
like a Highland earthquake,
I know that it's just ye a-gigglin'."

"Like a splutterin' bagpipe in need of a squeeze,
'neath me armpit, ye fit nice and snug.
Yer lumpy, yer dumpy,
yer've no' got much mould,
like the last sack o' spuds that I dug.

With a temper like thunder, ye boom and ye flash,
yer me rain, me drizzle, me snow.
Like a dinghy that's moored to a ruddy great post,
you're there, where'er I go."

Huddled beneath the dripping branches of a tall pine tree, nine gloomy Highland chieftains wrapped their kilts tightly around their bony knees and glared at each other.

Fingus the Wee's eyebrows were quivering again, mostly with the cold, but with as much venom as he could muster, too. "OCH, RUFUS, YOU'RE A WALLYDRAIGLE!" he roared. A shower of spit and splutter mingled with the freezing rain that fell relentlessly on the men.

Bogie Duntroon wriggled around on the pine needles, trying to find a spot where rivulets of water wouldn't swirl up inside his flapping kilt. "Aye, a wallydraigle an' a bletherskate!"

Lochless McDilly sneezed so hard that he sprayed green slime all over his sporran.

In unison, Duntroon, Macrascal, McSlimy, McDilly, Campbell, MacSnortle, McCrackle and Wee glared at McLean with quivering right eyebrows that looked like a sea of half-drowned furry caterpillars that had crawled their way out of a swamp. "We should've known it'd ne'er work," complained Fingus the Wee. "Now it'll be weeks before our wives let us back inside the castle walls."

Lochless McDilly sneezed again. "Mrs McDilly's forbidden me to open me restaurants an' all," he said dejectedly. "I've had to sell me ideas for the Big McDilly and Scottish Fries Meal to that Macdonald chieftain down south."

"I'm sorry," said Rufus McLean. "I was only tryin' to help. We should've just stuck to being haggis-rustlers, pick-sporrans and oatcake-smugglers. That's what we're good at."

"Yer a numpty," growled Bogie Duntroon. "We're all numpties."

A damp wind swirled around the pine tree and shook another shower of droplets from the needles.

Squeezing and squirming on the sodden, mossy ground, Duntroon, Macrascal, McSlimy, McDilly, Campbell, MacSnortle, McCrackle, McLean and Wee grimaced, wrinkled their noses and furrowed their foreheads. They settled in for a long, cold night.

And, as they all drifted off to sleep, each of the men was thinking the same thing:

"Thank goodness we only have to be romantic one day o' the year!"

Romantic:
no EQUIVALENT
Highland TERM
known